BAKE, MAKE & LEARN TO COOK

Fun & Healthy Recipes for Young Cooks

David Atherton

illustrated by Rachel Stubbs

CANDLEWICK PRESS

For my dream team: Nik, Kimberley, and Mum.
This book is as much them as me.
DA

For Rowan, Remy, Poppi, Maisy, and Ami—the chefs of our future.
With thanks to Jonathan for making me laugh and keeping me fed.
RS

• First US edition 2021 • Library of Congress Catalog Card Number pending • ISBN 978-1-5362-1936-4 • This book was typeset in Alice and WB Rachel Stubbs. The illustrations were done in ink and graphite and finished digitally.
Candlewick Press, 99 Dover Street, Somerville, Massachusetts 02144 • www.candlewick.com
Printed in Humen, Dongguan, China • 21 22 23 24 25 26 APS 10 9 8 7 6 5 4 3 2 1

Introduction

I loved my first cookbook. I remember taking turns with my twin brother to pick a recipe, and my mum was always on hand to help us. For my family, food wasn't a chore; it was a time to explore and have fun together. It also taught me valuable lessons about creating tasty dishes for other people.

There are so many different ingredients that can be used to make delicious food, and some of these, like fruits and vegetables, are packed with stuff that is good for our bodies as well as our taste buds. I think it's really important to eat healthy food when we can, to make sure we grow strong. You may be surprised to find recipes in this book such as a cake made with avocado, or brownies made with sweet potato, but you'll be even more surprised at how yummy they are.

For me, cooking is all about experimenting with new flavors and recipes, and I want you to feel free to put your own twist on the recipes in this book. Whether it's adding honey to slices of cake or jazzing up oatmeal with fruit or spices, go for flavor combinations your family and friends will love and be as creative as you like! Don't worry if things don't turn out perfectly; they will still taste delicious.

I started cooking when I was very young, and I still get excited about trying out new recipes. I hope you learn something with each dish you create and find recipes that soon become favorites. Recipes that inspire you to tie your apron and dance around the kitchen while creating amazing food!

David

Contents

Delicious Treats

Cakes and Bakes

A Quick Equipment List

This is the equipment you will use in this book:

parchment paper   cake pan   cookie sheet   cookie cutters   blender

safety knife   cutting board   strainer   cooling rack

frying pan (non-stick)   grater   mixing bowl   juicer

measuring cups   mixer   cupcake tin (12-hole)   peeler   rolling pin

saucepan   sieve   spatula   spoon   whisk

A couple of the recipes also use a stick blender or food processor.
Remember to always ask an adult to help!

Cooking Terms

beat: use a whisk or spoon to quickly mix the ingredients until they are well combined

cream: soften the ingredients by mixing them together to make a smooth paste

cut out: press a cookie cutter into the dough, wiggle it a little, and release it to make shapes

dust: use your fingers or a sieve to sprinkle a little flour onto a tray or powdered sugar on top of a cake

grease: use some parchment paper or a paper towel to wipe a little butter or oil on the inner sides of a pan

knead: give the dough a good bash and stretch it with your hands

line (a pan): cut some parchment paper to the same size as the pan, then press it in

roll: roll a rolling pin over the dough to make it flatter

rub: pick up little bits of the mix and rub it through your fingers until all of the mix looks like breadcrumbs

sift: tap the side of the sieve until the ingredients fall through into a bowl

spread: use a knife or spatula to move the mix around until it fills a pan or the top of a cake

Measurements

- Tsp = teaspoon
- Tbsp = tablespoon
- A pinch of something is the amount of an ingredient that you can pick up between your finger and thumb.
- The oven temperatures are in degrees Fahrenheit (°F).

Before You Get Going

Before you turn the page, read these handy tips:

- All the recipes in this book will need adult supervision, but it is so good to work together and have fun!

- It takes time to learn how to be safe in the kitchen. Make sure an adult helps you when using a knife, and always wear oven mitts to protect your hands when handling anything hot.

- Some of the recipes use specific baking pans and even things like ice pop molds or silicone mats. It's a good idea to check that you have all the equipment and ingredients needed for a recipe before you start.

- When it says "milk" in this book, the choice is yours. I usually use plant-based milks.

The same goes for vegetable spreads or butters. Make the recipes your own.

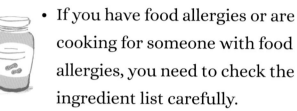

- If you have food allergies or are cooking for someone with food allergies, you need to check the ingredient list carefully.

- Finally, I am a nurse, so it is especially important for me to remind you to wash and dry your hands before you begin cooking and after handling any raw meat.

Starting the Day

Purple Smoothies

When I was a kid and I opened a packet of candies, everyone always wanted the purple ones. This smoothie is for them! The blueberries in this recipe give it the purple color, but you can also add a handful of red cabbage to make the color even deeper.

Method

1 Peel the banana and put it in the freezer for at least 3 hours. (I always have bananas in the freezer ready.)

2 Pour the blueberries, honey, and milk into a blender and blend.

3 Add the banana and keep blending until completely smooth.

4 Divide between 2 glasses.

Ingredients

1 banana
½ cup frozen blueberries
1 tbsp honey
1 cup milk

Makes 2 servings

Oatmeal Toppers

I have this breakfast every weekday morning. It warms you up on cold days and gives you energy until lunchtime. I've given you three of my favorite ideas to flavor the oatmeal, but you can try all kinds of toppings until you find your best one.

Ingredients

2 cups milk

1 cup rolled oats

1 tbsp honey

1 tsp tahini

A handful of slivered almonds and extra honey to top

Makes 2 servings

Method

1 Put the milk, oats, and honey into a saucepan.

2 Warm over a medium heat, stirring continuously with a wooden spoon.

3 When it starts to bubble, keep stirring.

4 Once the oatmeal is thick, spoon into 2 bowls.

5 Top with a teaspoon of tahini, a squirt of honey, and a few slivered almonds.

Here are two more of my favorite flavors:

Add 1 tsp turmeric and 1 tsp cinnamon to the oatmeal while stirring. Top with a handful of blueberries.

Add a mashed banana to the oatmeal while stirring, then top with sliced banana when it's in the bowls.

Ingredients

2 very ripe bananas
2 medium eggs
⅔ cup milk
2 tbsp maple syrup
2 tbsp vegetable oil
½ cup baby spinach leaves
1 ¾ cups all-purpose flour
1 tsp baking powder
Extra bananas,
    blueberries, and syrup
    for decoration

Makes 8 pancakes

Banana Bear Pancakes

These fluffy pancakes taste like bananas, look like cuddly bear faces, and are a great green start to the day. Adding spinach to the batter gives them their fun greenish color and also adds vitamins to the mix. To make the bear faces, I like to add a banana slice for the nose and blueberries for the eyes. Then I pour maple syrup all over the face. Yum!

Method

1 Blend the bananas, eggs, milk, maple syrup, oil, and spinach in a blender until very smooth.

2 Put the flour and baking powder in a large bowl.

3 Add the liquid from the blender and mix until combined.

4 Chill in the fridge for 30 minutes.

5 Lightly grease a large frying pan and put over a medium heat. Pour in a circle of batter and then add smaller circles for ears.

6 Allow to cook for 2 minutes, until bubbles cover the surface. Flip and cook for another minute on the other side.

7 Transfer to a plate. Continue until you have a stack of bears.

8 Use a slice of banana for the nose and blueberries for the eyes. Drizzle with a little maple syrup.

Edible Chia Bowls

This recipe is clever because you make little bowls that you can also eat! Once you've made your bowls, fill them with whatever you want. I've suggested fruit, yogurt, and squiggles of honey, but you could make them even fancier by adding melted chocolate, too.

Ingredients

¼ cup honey

2 tbsp butter (plus a little extra to grease the tin)

1 cup rolled oats

¼ cup flaked coconut

¼ cup chia seeds

1 tsp ground cinnamon

1 large container of plain yogurt

Extra blueberries, raspberries, and honey for decoration

Makes 12 servings

Method

1 In a small saucepan, melt the butter with the honey over a low heat.

2 Put the oats, coconut, chia seeds, and cinnamon into a bowl and mix.

3 Pour in the honey and butter mixture and stir until combined.

4 Grease a 12-hole muffin tin with a little butter, then put a large spoonful of mix into each hole and press with the back of the spoon to create a dip.

5 Let them sit for 1 hour in the fridge and go play.

6 Preheat oven to 350°F.

7 Bake for 15 minutes, then leave until fully cooled before gently removing from the tin.

8 Fill with yogurt, then add fruit and a squiggle of honey on top.

Craveable Corn Bites

When it's cold outside, you want something warm, sweet, and soft for breakfast. These are great dipped in your favorite sauce—mine is ketchup. You might want to make double the amount with this recipe, as once you start eating it's hard to stop going back for more!

Ingredients

1 large sweet potato

1 medium carrot

1 cup canned corn (whole kernel)

1 medium egg

A pinch of salt

A little vegetable oil

Makes 12 corn bites

Method

1 Preheat oven to 400°F.

2 Peel and chop the sweet potato and carrot into chunks. Boil in a saucepan for 10 minutes.

3 Drain and blend until smooth.

4 Scoop mixture into a mixing bowl. Add the corn, egg, and salt and combine.

5 Grease a 12-hole muffin tin with a little vegetable oil.

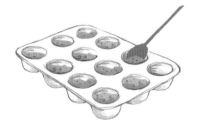

6 Spoon in the mix to half fill each hole.

7 Bake for 20 minutes. Allow to cool before eating.

Scrambled Egg Surprise!

Ingredients

¼ cup quinoa

3 medium eggs

A pinch of salt

A pinch of baking
powder

1 tbsp olive oil

Makes 2 servings

Scrambled eggs are so easy to make—you whisk all the ingredients together and it can't go wrong. These eggs have a surprise ingredient of quinoa to give them a bit more bite, but you can add lots of other ingredients, like chopped veggies or grated cheese, to make them even more special. Once your scrambled egg surprise is ready, spoon it over a piece of hot-buttered toast to serve.

Method

1 Rinse the quinoa, then cook in boiling water—as per cooking instructions—and leave to cool.

2 Whisk the eggs with the salt and baking powder.

3 Drain the cooked quinoa and add to the egg mixture.

4 Add the olive oil to a frying pan over a medium heat.

5 Pour in the eggs and stir continuously until just cooked, then serve.

Nutty French Toast

This is one of my favorite breakfasts—the flavor combo of banana and peanut butter is THE BEST! Stale bread actually works better than fresh bread for this recipe. You'll also need a really good nonstick frying pan as the French toast can get a little sticky.

Ingredients

1 very ripe banana

6 slices of stale bread

A jar of peanut butter

2 medium eggs

¼ cup milk

1 tbsp honey

A little butter to grease the pan

Method

Makes 3 sandwiches

1 Mash the banana on a plate.

2 Spread one slice of bread with one-third of the mashed banana.

3 Spread another slice with some peanut butter and sandwich together. Repeat to make 2 more sandwiches.

4 Whisk the eggs, milk, and honey together in a wide-bottomed bowl.

5 Place the first sandwich in the bowl for 30 seconds.

6 Flip it over, leave for 10 seconds, and put aside. Repeat steps 5 and 6 for the other 2 sandwiches.

7 Lightly grease the frying pan and put over a medium heat.

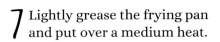

8 Fry the sandwich for 3 minutes. (Don't have the heat too high or it'll burn.)

9 Flip the sandwich over and fry for another 3 minutes. Repeat steps 7–9 for the other 2 sandwiches.

10 Carefully place each sandwich onto a plate, cut in half, and drizzle with honey.

Breakfast Jars

If you're up early for a dance class or a team practice and you need something speedy, this is the perfect go-to breakfast. You prepare it the night before in jars so you can eat it on the go the next day. You can experiment with the flavors, but cinnamon and honey is my favorite.

Ingredients

1 cup rolled oats

¼ cup chia seeds

1 tsp ground cinnamon

1 Granny Smith apple

1 cup milk

1 tsp honey

A handful of grapes
(chopped in half)

Makes 4 servings

Method

1 Mix the oats, chia seeds, and cinnamon in a bowl.

2 Grate the apple into the bowl, then add milk, honey, and grapes and stir.

3 Divide the mixture equally between 4 jars, screw the lids back on, and put in the fridge overnight.

4 To serve, you can add yogurt, fruit, or any topping you would like.

Lunches and Simple Suppers

Magic Tomato Sauce

This tomato sauce is made from lots of different vegetables. It's magic because it can be made ahead of time, ready to be used for so many different meals—including several of the recipes in this book. Try adding some to your favorite pasta or veggie noodles. It makes so many meals magic!

Ingredients

Two 15 oz cans of
　　diced tomatoes
¼ cup water
1 onion
1 medium carrot
2 sticks of celery
½ a green pepper
5 cloves of garlic
1 tsp salt

Makes 2 portions

Method

1 Pour both cans of tomatoes into a medium saucepan and add the water. Bring to a simmer over a medium heat.

2 Peel the onion and carrot and roughly chop along with the celery and pepper, then add to the saucepan.

3 Finely grate the garlic and add this with the salt.

4 Simmer for 30 minutes over a medium heat, then pour into a blender and whizz until smooth. Leave to cool.

5 Divide into 2 portions and keep in the fridge for up to 3 days, or freeze.

Teapot Soup

Who says you need to eat your soup from a bowl? I think you can drink soup like a hot cup of tea, so I pour mine from a teapot and drink it from a mug to make it more fun. You can even serve it at a tea party for your friends and family.

Ingredients

½ cup split red lentils

2 bouillon cubes

1 portion of magic
tomato sauce

1 tsp ground cumin

2 tsp garam masala

1 tsp ground cinnamon

1 tsp turmeric powder

4 slices of bread

Makes 4 servings

Method

1 Simmer the lentils in a saucepan with 3 ½ cups of boiling water and the bouillon cubes for 10 minutes.

2 Add the magic tomato sauce and spices, stir, and simmer for another 10 minutes over a medium heat.

3 Pour into a blender and blend until smooth. Transfer to a teapot that has a wide spout.

4 Cut the bread into cubes and put in a small bowl.

5 Pour the soup into 4 mugs and spoon the bread on top like sugar cubes.

Ingredients

2 ½ cups all-purpose flour

2 tsp salt

2 tsp sweet paprika

2 tsp fast-acting yeast

1 medium carrot

¼ cup milk

½ cup warm water

Coarse cornmeal and
poppy seeds to decorate

1 red pepper

16 raisins

Makes 8 breadsticks

Snaky Breadsticks

I love making bread because you can bash it around with your hands. The dough can be tricky to roll out, but don't rush, and eventually you'll get a lovely long (and a little scary-looking) snake. Remember that your snake will rise in the oven, so you need to make them very thin, but you can twist them into any shape you want. I like to make the breadsticks swim in some soup—teapot soup goes well with this recipe—before I bite the heads off.

Method

1 Put the flour, salt, paprika, and yeast in a mixing bowl.

2 Peel and finely grate the carrot.

3 Mix the carrot, milk, and water in a cup.

4 Pour the carrot mixture into the bowl and stir until you have a sticky dough.

5 Cover with a damp cloth for 10 minutes.

6 Knead the dough on a floured surface for 5 minutes. (It may be sticky, but don't add any more flour.)

7 Put it back in the bowl and cover with a damp cloth until it has doubled in size. (This may take up to an hour.)

8 Preheat oven to 325°F.

9 Punch all the air out and divide into 8 pieces.

10 Dust your worktop with flour and use your hands to roll a piece of dough into a long, thin sausage.

11 Sprinkle some poppy seeds and cornmeal onto a plate and then roll your bread snake in it.

12 Choose one end to be the head, cut a little mouth with scissors, and add a tongue made from red pepper. Add raisins for eyes.

13 Shape the snakes on cookie sheets lined with parchment paper. Leave for 10 minutes and then bake for 8–10 minutes until golden brown.

Piggy Buns

These buns are wonderfully soft and are perfect for sandwiches. Once you've baked the piggies, arrange them on a plate to make a pigsty. If you like, you can make other animals, too—I'm going to try a monkey next. What's your favorite animal?

Ingredients

3 cups white
    bread flour
1 tsp fast-acting yeast
1 tsp salt
1 cup warm water
A handful of green
    olives to decorate

Makes 12 buns

Method

1 Put the flour, yeast, and salt into a mixing bowl.

2 Add the warm water and mix with a spatula until it just comes to a dough.

3 Cover with a damp cloth and leave for 15 minutes.

4 Knead the dough for 15 minutes. It will be quite sticky at the start, but try not to use any extra flour at this stage.

5 Cover again with the damp cloth and leave to rise until it doubles in size.

6 Turn out onto a floured surface, knead for 10 seconds, then divide into 12 pieces.

7 Pull off a small piece for the nose—about the size of a marble—and roll the rest into a ball.

8 Place on a tray lined with parchment paper. Roll the nose into a ball and stick on top.

9 Chop an olive into little pieces, then push 2 pieces, hard, into the nose and add 2 pieces for eyes.

10 Once the buns are complete, leave them on baking trays to rise until they double in size.

11 Preheat oven to 400°F.

12 Use scissors to make 2 snips on top of each bun for the ears, then bake for 12 minutes.

Ingredients

Tortillas

1 ¼ cups all-purpose flour
⅓ cup whole wheat flour
A pinch of salt
2 tbsp butter (diced)
½ cup water

Taco filling

½ lb ground beef
1 tsp ground cumin
1 tsp paprika
1 can of kidney beans (15 oz)
1 portion of magic tomato
   sauce (p. 14)
A pinch of salt
Wedges of lime to garnish

Makes 12 tacos

Tasty Tacos

It takes time to make your own tortillas, but it's fun and they taste SO nice! If you don't have time, don't worry; the recipe still works with store-bought tortillas. Either way, you can add lots of toppings to your tacos, like grated cheese, tomato salsa, guacamole, and sour cream, to make them even tastier.

Method

1 Put the flours and a pinch of salt in a bowl and rub in the butter until the mixture resembles breadcrumbs.

2 Pour in the water and mix to make a dough. (It may be sticky, but don't add any more flour.)

3 Cover the bowl with a damp cloth to keep the dough soft.

4 Leave this to rest for 1 hour.

5 Gently fry the ground beef over a medium heat until browned.

6 Add the cumin and paprika and fry for another minute. Drain the kidney beans.

7 Add the beans, tomato sauce, and a pinch of salt and simmer for 10 minutes, then set aside.

8 Divide the dough into 12 pieces. Take a piece of dough and roll into a ball.

9 Sprinkle a clean surface with flour, then roll out one ball until very thin.

10 Heat a frying pan to a medium-high heat and dry fry the flattened dough for 1 minute on each side.

11 Continue with the rest of the dough, covering the finished tortillas with a clean tea towel.

12 Put a spoonful of the filling on each tortilla and fold in half.

13 Serve with a wedge of lime.

Ingredients

1 onion

1 tsp olive oil

2 peppers

2 portions of magic
tomato sauce (p. 14)

1 small sweet potato

A pinch of salt

1 mozzarella ball

1 bunch of basil

1 box of no-boil lasagna
sheets

4 oz cheddar cheese

Makes 6 servings

The BEST Veggie Lasagna

Lasagna was the first proper meal I made by myself, and I was so proud! I still love making it today. The fun here is in the assembly. The best thing about this dinner is that you can experiment by adding all kinds of different vegetables in step 2 of the recipe, or you can add some ground meat in step 5 to turn it into a meaty dish.

Method

1 Peel and finely chop the onion. Place in a large frying pan with a little olive oil and gently fry for 5 minutes.

2 Dice the peppers, add to the pan, and fry over a medium heat for a further 10 minutes, until soft.

3 Add the tomato sauce and stir.

4 Peel the sweet potato and grate into the pan.

5 Add the salt and simmer for 15 minutes.

6 Preheat oven to 400°F.

7 Add one-third of the sauce to a large baking dish.

8 Chop the mozzarella ball into small chunks and add half to the dish with some basil leaves.

9 Place a single layer of lasagna sheets on top.

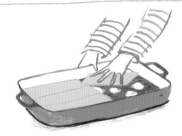

10 Repeat steps 7–9.

11 Add the rest of the tomato sauce.

12 Grate the cheddar cheese and sprinkle on top of the lasagna.

13 Bake for 40 minutes.

Ingredients

1 onion

1 tsp vegetable oil

3 cloves of garlic

A chunk of ginger root (½ inch)

1 tsp ground cumin

1 tsp coriander powder

1 tsp turmeric powder

½ tsp ground black pepper

1 tsp salt

1 can of diced tomatoes (15 oz)

1 cup water

¾ lb boneless, skinless
   chicken thighs

1 ½ cups frozen peas

1 cup jasmine rice

Makes 4 servings

Happy Curry

Take my word for it: curries are so, so tasty, and I'm always really happy when I get to eat this curry! I like to make little smiley faces with some peas before serving it to my friends and family.

Method

1 Peel and finely chop the onion. Add to a large frying pan with the oil and gently fry over a medium heat.

2 Peel and finely grate the garlic and ginger. Add to the pan along with the spices and salt. Fry for 2 minutes.

3 Add the can of diced tomatoes and 1 cup water and simmer for 15 minutes.

4 Cut the chicken into bite-size pieces using kitchen scissors and add to the sauce.

5 Simmer gently for 10 minutes, then stir and simmer for another 15 minutes.

6 Simmer the peas for 5 minutes in boiling water, then drain and set aside.

7 Put the rice into a small saucepan and cover with boiling water to just above the rice level.

8 Put over a medium heat. As soon as you see the first bubbles of a simmer, put on a tight-fitting lid and turn down to lowest heat.

9 Leave the rice for 12 minutes and do not remove the lid.

10 Add two-thirds of the peas to the sauce and divide between 4 bowls.

11 Press a quarter of the rice into a ladle—really squash it down—and place in the middle of each bowl of curry.

12 Make a smiley face and hair with the extra peas.

Ingredients

3 cups bread flour

1 tsp fast-acting yeast

1 tsp salt

1 ½ tbsp olive oil

1 cup warm water

½ a portion of magic tomato
   sauce (p. 14)

Dried oregano

1 ball of mozzarella

Sliced black olives for
   decorating

Makes 4 pizzas

Octo-Pizzas

Making pizza is great because everyone can decide what toppings they want (although I wouldn't suggest a banana!). These pizzas are octopus-shaped. The body is the main pizza and the tentacles are breadsticks—perfect for tearing off and dipping into any leftover magic sauce.

Method

1 Put the flour, yeast, and salt into a large mixing bowl.

2 Pour in the oil and water and mix with a spatula to make a dough.

3 Cover with a damp cloth and leave for 5 minutes.

4 Knead the dough in the bowl for 5 minutes. It will be very sticky—don't worry if it sticks to your hands.

5 Cover and leave in a warm place until it doubles in size. (This may take over an hour.)

6 Preheat oven to 400°F.

7 Place the dough onto a floured surface and gently knead until it goes back to its original size.

8 Divide into 4 pieces.

9 Roll out each piece to a circle ¼ inch thick. You can also use your hands to stretch it a little.

10 Transfer the pieces to a lined baking tray.

11 Divide the bottom half of the dough into 8 sections, then shape them into legs.

12 Cover each pizza with the tomato sauce and sprinkle with oregano.

13 Dot the body with mozzarella pieces. Place black olive slices for eyes and for suckers along the tentacles.

14 Leave the pizzas to rest for 5 minutes, then bake for 12 minutes until golden.

27

Ingredients

1 large carrot

1 lb russet potatoes

¼ cup milk

2 oz cheddar cheese

1 can of tuna (5 oz)

¼ cup frozen peas

1 medium egg

1 cup breadcrumbs
(panko are
crunchiest)

Black olives to decorate

Makes 6 hedgehogs

Crunchy Hedgehogs

These cute hedgehogs are crispy on the outside and creamy and soft on the inside—and even have a tasty surprise in the center. If you're feeling adventurous, flavor the mashed potato with a sprinkle of cumin or turmeric to make them even tastier. You can make as many different animal shapes as you like!

Method

1 Peel and chop the carrot and simmer in salted water for 10 minutes.

2 Peel and chop the potatoes.

3 Add to the saucepan and simmer for 10 minutes, until carrots and potatoes are soft, then drain.

4 Keep back 2 tsp of milk and mash the rest with the potatoes and carrots.

5 Grate half the cheese into the mix and leave to cool for 30 minutes.

6 Preheat oven to 375°F.

7 Take a handful of the mix and make a ball. Flatten it slightly.

8 Add 1/2 tsp tuna, a few peas, and a pinch of grated cheese to the middle. Squash the sides together to make a ball again.

9 Place on a tray lined with parchment paper and pinch out the nose.

10 Beat the egg with the rest of the milk.

11 Brush the hedgehogs with the egg mixture and sprinkle with breadcrumbs.

12 Cut the olives into pieces and place as eyes and a nose.

13 Bake for 50 minutes, or until golden and crispy.

Ingredients

1 box of pasta (whichever shape you like)

2 portions of magic tomato sauce (p. 14)

1 head of broccoli

1 ½ cups frozen peas

1 bunch of basil

2 tsp dried oregano

A pinch of salt and pepper

4 oz cheddar cheese

Makes 6 servings

Perfect Pasta Bake

This is your chance to perfect your own signature pasta bake. Mine has broccoli, peas, basil, and oregano in it, but you can choose whatever fillings you want. You can also choose your favorite pasta shape. I like spaghetti because it looks like worms when it's cooked—and it's messy and fun to eat!

Method

1 Boil the pasta as per cooking instructions and drain.

2 Put the tomato sauce into a large bowl and add the cooked pasta.

3 Preheat oven to 400°F.

4 Chop the broccoli into florets, then simmer for 10 minutes. Drain and add to pasta.

5 Add the frozen peas, tear in the basil, and sprinkle in the oregano and a pinch of salt and pepper.

6 Mix together and transfer to a large baking dish.

7 Grate the cheese and sprinkle on top.

8 Bake for 20 minutes or until the cheese is golden and bubbling on top.

Ingredients

1 medium sweet potato

1 baking potato

2 oz cheddar cheese

1 medium egg

1 tsp salt

½ cup frozen peas

2 tbsp tomato paste

1 package of filo pastry

A little olive oil

Makes 10 potpies

Easy-Peasy Potpies

These potpies look fancy, but they are actually very easy to make. I've used potato, peas, and cheese in this recipe, but you can use a mix of any tasty ingredients you'd like. Whichever ingredients you choose, there's nothing better than a hot potpie to warm you up on a cold day.

Method

1 Peel and finely grate both potatoes, and grate the cheese. Mix together in a bowl.

2 Add the egg, salt, peas, and tomato paste and stir until combined.

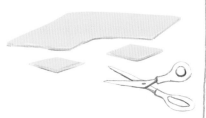

3 Use scissors to cut the filo pastry into quarters (roughly 6x6-inch squares).

4 Preheat oven to 375°F.

5 Brush 10 holes of a muffin tin with a little olive oil. Place a pastry square in one hole, then add 2 more layers.

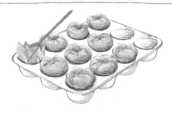

6 Put a tablespoon of mixture in the middle of the pie and fold the excess pastry over the top. Repeat steps 5 and 6 to make 9 more pies.

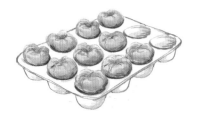

7 Brush with a little olive oil, then bake for 15 minutes.

8 Leave the pies to cool on a cooling rack, then enjoy! Freeze any leftover pies for another day.

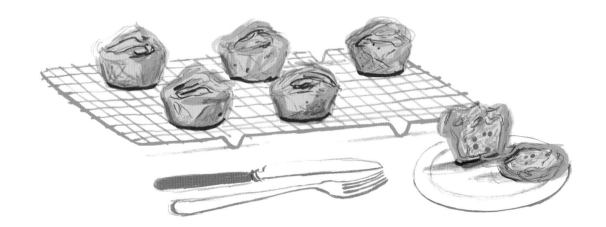

Veggie Hot Dogs

These cheesy hot dogs can be made for a party, thrown on the BBQ, or simply enjoyed as a dinnertime treat. They go nicely inside piggy buns (see page 18) with a good dollop of your favorite sauce to top them off.

Ingredients

1 can of red kidney beans (15 oz)

3 oz extra-firm tofu

1 medium sweet potato

2 oz cheddar cheese

2 tbsp all-purpose flour

A pinch of salt

1 tsp smoked paprika

1 medium egg

1 tbsp olive oil

6 hot dog buns

Makes 6 hot dogs

Method

1 Drain and rinse the beans, then pour into a food processor and pulse to break them up a bit.

2 Mash the tofu in a bowl with a fork.

3 Peel and finely grate the sweet potato, then add to the bowl.

4 Grate in the cheddar cheese.

5 Add the flour, salt, paprika, and egg.

6 Smush with your hands until combined and then chill in the fridge for 30 minutes.

7 Divide into 6 portions, roll roughly, then place on a piece of wax paper. Dust with flour and finish rolling to make neat hot dogs.

8 Chill hot dogs in the fridge for 1 hour.

9 Pour the olive oil into a frying pan and gently fry for 10–15 minutes, turning with tongs as you go.

10 Add a hot dog to a bun and top with your favorite sauce!

Ingredients

Satay sticks

2 cloves of garlic

A chunk of ginger root
(½ inch)

½ cup of coconut milk

2 tsp soy sauce

2 tsp maple syrup

14 oz package extra-firm
tofu

Dipping sauce

2 tbsp smooth peanut
butter

Juice of ½ a lime

1 tbsp soy sauce

1 clove of garlic
(optional)

3 tbsp coconut milk

Makes 12 servings

Satay Sticks

Satay sauce is usually made with peanuts (I LOVE peanuts), but you can make this recipe with other nut butters. I like to put my satay in a toasted pita pocket with a little salad and then dip the whole thing in the nutty dipping sauce.

Method

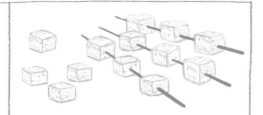

1 Put the garlic, ginger, coconut milk, soy sauce, and maple syrup into a blender and blend until completely smooth.

2 Carefully cut the tofu into 1-inch cubes. Thread onto 12 skewers.

3 Pour the marinade over the cubes and refrigerate for at least 1 hour. Preheat oven to 400°F.

4 Transfer to 2 lined baking sheets and bake for 45 minutes. Leave to cool a little, then carefully move the skewers onto a plate.

5 Blend all the dipping sauce ingredients until smooth. You may need to add more coconut milk to get a saucy consistency.

6 Dip in a piece of tofu and enjoy!

Delicious
Treats

Veggie Summer Rolls

These refreshing and crunchy rolls are perfect for a summer evening. These are particularly cool because you can see the colorful vegetables from the outside. If you want to make this recipe vegetarian, just leave out the fish sauce and it will still be super-tasty.

Ingredients

Dipping sauce

3 tbsp smooth peanut butter

2 tbsp lime juice

4 tsp soy sauce

1 clove of garlic (optional)

2 tsp fish sauce

1 tsp honey

Rolls

½ an iceberg lettuce

1 medium carrot

½ a cucumber

½ package rice noodles (4 oz)

10 6-inch rice paper wrappers

Cilantro leaves

Basil leaves

Makes 10 rolls

Method

1 Put all the ingredients for the dipping sauce into a blender and whizz until smooth.

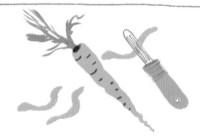

2 Add some water if it's a bit thick.

3 Shred the lettuce into fine strips.

4 Peel the carrot, then keep using the peeler to make ribbons.

5 Slice the cucumber into thin sticks.

6 Put the rice noodles into a bowl and soak in boiling water for 10 minutes.

7 Drain and set aside.

8 Put a rice wrapper into a bowl of warm water for 15 seconds. Take out and dry on a tea towel.

9 Move wrapper to a damp chopping board. Place noodles, lettuce, carrot strips, cucumber sticks, cilantro, and basil leaves in the middle and start to roll up.

10 Roll halfway, then fold in the ends and finish rolling. Continue with the rest of the rice wrappers. Serve with the peanut dipping sauce.

Ingredients

1 cup sushi rice

1 cup cold water

¼ cup rice vinegar

1 ½ tbsp sugar

A pinch of salt

3–4 sheets of nori seaweed

½ a cucumber

A handful of sesame seeds

A little soy sauce

Makes 10 rolls

Sushi Shapes

Making sushi is a sticky business, but lots of fun. You can use any shaped cookie cutter you like for this recipe—the more sushi shapes, the better! I like to decorate the sushi shapes with cucumber and sesame seeds, but you can use any crunchy veggies before dipping it all in soy sauce.

Method

1 Rinse the sushi rice in a sieve until water runs clear.

2 Soak in cold water for 15 minutes, then drain.

3 Put the rice in a saucepan with the cup of water and bring to a simmer. Put on a tight-fitting lid and turn down to lowest heat.

4 Leave for 15 minutes without removing lid.

5 Take off the heat and leave for another 10 minutes without removing lid.

6 Mix the vinegar, sugar, and salt until the sugar and salt have dissolved.

7 Pour over the rice and stir though.

8 Leave to cool and go play!

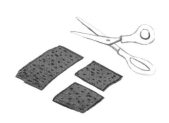

9 Cut the nori seaweed into squares just bigger than your cookie cutter.

10 Rub some water onto a cutting board. Tip out the sushi rice and press down with wet hands until it is about ¼ inch in thickness.

11 Dip the cookie cutter in water and cut shapes out of the rice.

12 Place a rice shape on top of each seaweed square.

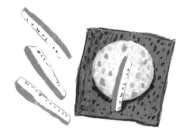

13 Slice the cucumber into sticks and place on top.

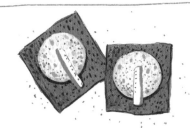

14 Sprinkle with sesame seeds and serve drizzled with a little soy sauce.

Ingredients

1 large sweet potato

1 clove of garlic

3 tsp tahini

1 tsp salt

½ tsp smoked paprika

½ tsp ground cumin

Juice of ½ a lime

Serves 4

Sweet and Spicy Dip

This is one of my favorite go-to treats. It's delicious on its own, and it can be eaten hot or cold. I like to dip pita bread into it, or spread a lovely thick layer on some toast and sprinkle with seeds.

Method

1 Bake the sweet potato for 45 minutes at 400°F, then allow to cool. (You can do this ahead of time.)

2 Scoop out the sweet potato flesh and put in a bowl. Mash with a fork.

3 Finely grate or crush the garlic and add to the bowl.

4 Add the tahini, salt, paprika, cumin, and lime juice and mix together with a fork.

5 Serve with toasted pita bread.

Hummus Lion

Making hummus is so easy. It's super-quick to whizz all the ingredients together and it's so tasty! I like to decorate the hummus with chopped olives to make a fun lion face and to add a carrot stick mane that everyone can use to dip into the tasty hummus.

Ingredients

4–5 carrots
1 can of chickpeas (15 oz)
1 clove of garlic
1 tsp salt
1 ½ tbsp olive oil
3 tsp tahini
Juice of ½ a lemon
Black olives to decorate

Serves 4

Method

1 Peel the carrots and carefully slice into carrot sticks.

2 Drain the chickpeas but save 3 tbsp of the water from the can.

3 Crush the garlic and mix with the salt, olive oil, and tahini.

4 In a food processor, blend the chickpeas with the chickpea water and lemon juice.

5 Add half the oil mixture and blend again. Then add the second half and blend until smooth.

6 Put the hummus in the middle of a plate and arrange the carrot sticks around it. Chop the olives into little pieces and use them to make the face.

Fruity Jelly Jars

This recipe is all about using your favorite fruity flavors. You can choose any fruit juice and add whatever fruit pieces you like. You can even make layers of jellies with different colors; just let each layer set in the fridge before adding the next.

Ingredients

2 cups fruit juice
1 tsp agar powder
A selection of fruit

Makes 3 jars

Method

1 Pour the fruit juice into a small saucepan and sprinkle on the agar powder. Leave for 5 minutes.

2 Prepare your fruit by chopping it into any shapes you please. You could even use mini cookie cutters.

3 Slowly bring the fruit juice to a simmer over a medium heat while stirring.

4 Once all the agar powder has dissolved, pour into the clean jars, filling them halfway.

5 Add half of your fruit pieces.

6 Leave until cool, then add the rest of the fruit pieces.

7 Chill in the fridge for 1 hour.

8 Top with extra fruit if you wish.

Ingredients

⅓ cup banana chips
1 medium egg white
½ cup powdered sugar
1 cup sliced almonds
¼ cup raisins
1 tbsp poppy seeds

Makes 12 cookies

Banana Nut Florentines

These are sweet, chewy, and crunchy—all the best things!
If possible, use silicone mats for this recipe, as the florentines
will be so, so sticky and it's very hard to
get them off parchment paper.

Method

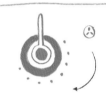

1 Preheat oven to 325°F.

2 Line 2 baking sheets with silicone mats.

3 Crush the banana chips into small pieces using a food processor. (Or you can put the chips into a little bag and bash with a rolling pin.)

4 Separate the egg white from the yolk through your fingers (you'll need two people for this).

5 Mix the egg white with the powdered sugar, crushed banana chips, almonds, and raisins.

6 Spoon a tablespoon full of mixture onto a silicone mat and press down flat.

7 Continue until all the mixture is used, then sprinkle with poppy seeds.

8 Bake for 10 minutes, or until golden. If pale, keep in the oven for another 2–3 minutes.

9 Once out of the oven, allow to cool completely before peeling off the mat.

Ingredients

1 cup rolled oats

2 oz dark chocolate

½ cup pitted dates

½ cup prunes

Sunflower seeds
   to decorate

Makes 8–10 stars

Energy Stars

These snacks are packed with natural energy—just like stars!—and are especially good to eat before you exercise. What's more, they're super-quick to make, as you don't have to bake them. Don't worry if you don't have a star-shaped cookie cutter; you can use any shape—they'll taste just as yummy.

Method

1 Blend the oats in a food processor for 10 seconds and set aside.

2 Melt the chocolate in a cup in the microwave, checking every 10 seconds, until just melted.

3 Blend the dates and prunes until you have a smooth paste.

4 Pour in the melted chocolate and blend again until very smooth and shiny.

5 Transfer to a bowl and knead in the oats.

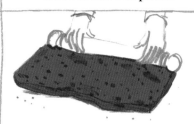

6 Roll out to roughly ¼ inch thick and cut out with a star-shaped cookie cutter.

7 Finally, add sunflower seeds on top for decoration.

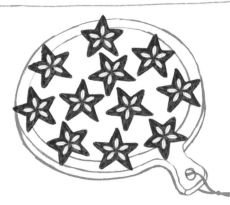

Ingredients

2 bananas

8 grapes (sliced in half)

10 strawberries

Makes 4 pops

Two-Tone Pops

You will always want some of these cool and colorful pops in the freezer after you've been playing outside on a hot, sunny day. You'll need an ice pop mold for this recipe to make sure the pops hold their shape and are ready to eat when you're ready to be cooled down.

Method

1 Put 1 banana into a cup or beaker and whizz with a stick blender until smooth.

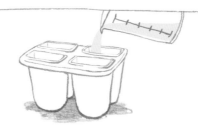

2 Pour into an ice pop mold to fill halfway. Push in 2 grape halves and freeze for 1 hour.

3 Whizz the second banana and the strawberries with a stick blender until smooth.

4 Fill up the ice pop molds and push in 2 more grapes.

5 Insert the pop sticks and place in the freezer for at least 3 hours.

6 Once frozen, take molds out of the freezer and run under some warm water to release the pops.

Ingredients

2 overripe bananas

½ cup Greek yogurt

2 tsp cocoa powder

1 tsp vanilla extract

Makes 2 servings

Ice-No-Cream

Here is an easy way to make your own chocolate banana ice cream, and it's a good way to use up any overripe bananas. It takes time to freeze the bananas, but I promise that it's worth it!

Method

1 Peel and slice the bananas, lay onto small baking sheets, and freeze for at least 3 hours.

2 Once frozen, put into a cup or beaker with the Greek yogurt, cocoa powder, and vanilla extract.

3 Blend with a stick blender until it has a smooth ice-cream consistency.

4 Quickly divide into 2 bowls and eat!

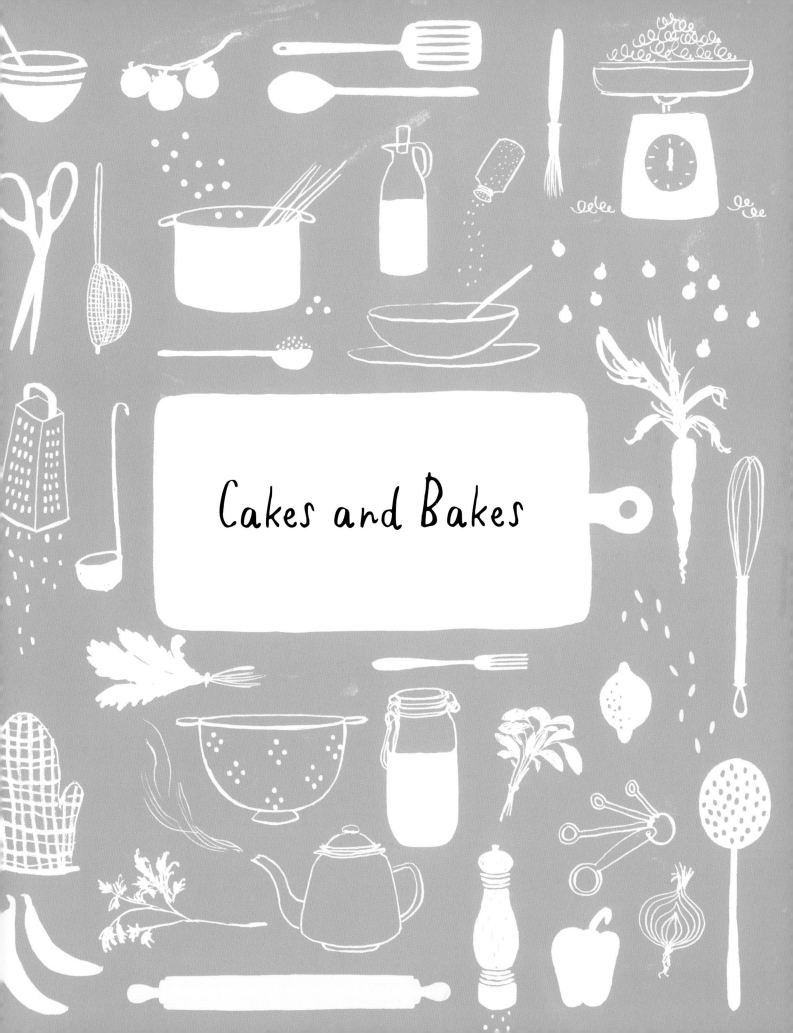

Cakes and Bakes

Ingredients

1 medium egg

¼ cup vegetable oil

¼ cup granulated sugar

1 ⅔ cups spinach leaves

½ a ripe banana

½ tsp vanilla extract

1 small zucchini

1 ¼ cups all-purpose
   flour

1 tsp baking powder

½ cup powdered sugar

2 tsp water

Lots of gummy candies
   to decorate

Makes 12 cupcakes

Cakey Caterpillar

This is my favorite birthday cake—I've had it for five different birthdays so far! I think the best way to decorate it is to put candies onto toothpicks, then stand two of them on each cake to make a very furry caterpillar. If you want to make the caterpillar even longer, just double the ingredients!

Method

1 Preheat oven to 350°F.

2 Prepare a 12-hole cupcake tin with cupcake wrappers.

3 In a blender, blend the eggs, oil, sugar, spinach, banana, and vanilla until smooth and green.

4 Finely grate ½ cup of zucchini.

5 Mix the flour with the baking powder in a large bowl.

6 Stir in the zucchini.

 **7** Add the blended ingredients and mix until combined.

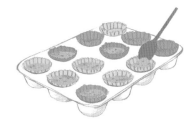 **8** Divide into cupcake wrappers (no more than two-thirds full).

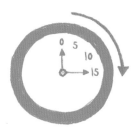 **9** Bake for 15 minutes, or until golden, then leave to cool on a cooling rack.

 **10** Put the powdered sugar in a clean bowl, add 2 tsp of water, and mix.

 **11** Once the cupcakes have cooled, top with the icing.

 **12** Arrange in a long, wriggly line and decorate with candy.

Carrot Cake

Carrot cake is moist and packed full of flavor. It's a little tricky to grate the carrots, but once you've made this cake I bet you'll want to bake it again and again. If you are making it for a special occasion, use a fork to make a swirly pattern in the icing and then sprinkle it all over with a pinch of cinnamon.

Ingredients

Cake

½ cup granulated sugar

½ cup brown sugar

¾ cup vegetable oil

3 medium eggs

3–4 medium carrots

1 ¼ cups all-purpose flour

2 tsp baking powder

1 tsp ground cinnamon

Icing

⅔ cup Greek yogurt

¾ cup powdered sugar

1 tsp vanilla extract

A pinch of cinnamon to decorate

Makes 12 servings

Method

1 Preheat oven to 350°F.

2 Grease and dust 2 8-inch round tins with flour.

3 Beat the granulated sugar, brown sugar, oil, and eggs until smooth.

4 Peel and finely grate the carrots—or whizz them in a food processor—and add to the bowl.

5 Mix in the flour, baking powder, and cinnamon.

6 Divide the mixture between the 2 tins and smooth the tops.

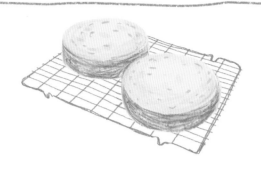

7 Bake for 25 minutes. Turn out onto a cooling rack and leave until completely cooled.

8 Put the yogurt, powdered sugar, and vanilla extract into a clean bowl and stir gently until just mixed.

9 Spread half the icing on one cake, then make a sandwich with the second cake. Decorate the top with the rest of the icing and a sprinkle of cinnamon.

Ingredients

Cake

2 ¼ cups all-purpose flour

2 cups granulated sugar

¼ cup cocoa powder

2 tsp baking powder

½ cup milk

½ cup vegetable oil

2 medium eggs

2 tsp vanilla extract

1 cup water

Icing

½ cup granulated sugar

½ cup cocoa powder

¼ cup corn starch

½ cup water

1 tsp vanilla extract

1 ½ tbsp butter

Makes 24 servings

Mega-Chocolatey Cake

This cake is mega-easy to make and it always comes out so soft and SO chocolatey. The icing is sticky and fudgy, and once it's spread over the cake, you can jazz it up by sprinkling even more grated chocolate on top.

Method

1 Preheat oven to 325°F.

2 Grease and dust a rectangular cake tin (13x9) with flour.

3 Mix the flour, sugar, cocoa powder, and baking powder together in a bowl.

4 In a separate bowl, beat the milk, oil, eggs, vanilla, and water.

5 Pour this into the flour mix and beat until smooth.

6 Pour into the cake tin.

7 Bake for 35–40 minutes, then leave to cool in the tin.

8 In a saucepan, mix the sugar, cocoa, corn starch, water, vanilla, and butter over a medium heat, stirring continuously until smooth. If lumpy, transfer to a blender and whizz until smooth.

9 Pour the icing over the cake and serve slices from the tin.

Sweetie Birthday Cake

Everyone wants a special cake for their birthday. This cake is a simple vanilla cake, but what could be more special than topping it with spoonfuls of creamy icing and as many of your favorite sweets as you can fit on the cake? It's party time!

Ingredients

Cake

2 ripe avocados

1 ¼ cups granulated sugar

4 medium eggs

2 tsp vanilla extract

2 cups self-rising flour

½ tsp baking powder

Icing

⅓ cup soft unsalted butter

2 cups powdered sugar

⅓ cup Greek yogurt

1 tsp vanilla extract

Your favorite sweets

Makes 12 servings

Method

1 Preheat oven to 325°F.

2 Grease and dust 2 8-inch round tins with flour.

3 Carefully remove the stones from the avocados, scoop the flesh into a bowl, and add sugar. Use a whisk to mix until smooth.

4 Beat in the eggs one at a time, then the vanilla.

5 Stir the flour and baking powder into the mix.

6 Divide into the 2 tins and smooth the tops.

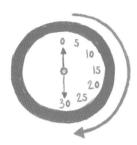

7 Bake for 30 minutes.

8 Turn out onto a cooling rack and leave until cooled.

9 Beat together the butter and half of the powdered sugar until smooth.

10 Add the Greek yogurt, vanilla, and the rest of the powdered sugar and whisk together until combined.

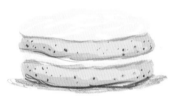

11 Spread half the icing on one cake, sandwich the two cakes together, and spread the rest of the icing on top.

12 Finish by topping with plenty of your favorite sweets.

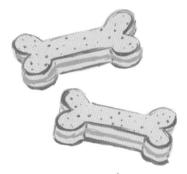

Ingredients

2 ⅓ cups all-purpose flour

½ cup granulated sugar

A pinch of baking powder

¼ cup unsalted butter (diced)

A jar of smooth peanut butter

1 medium egg

Makes 18 cookies

Peanut Butter Bones

I love dogs, and when I was a kid I used to pretend I *was* a dog. These cookies are for anyone who wants to have fun eating bone-shaped "biscuits," just like our furry friends! If you don't have a bone-shaped cutter, don't worry; any cutter will work—just use plenty of peanut butter to sandwich the cookies together.

Method

1 Combine the flour, sugar, and baking powder in a large mixing bowl.

2 Rub in the butter, then add ¼ cup of peanut butter. Continue until the mixture resembles breadcrumbs.

3 Add the egg and stir together to make a dough.

4 Wrap and put in the fridge for 1 hour while you go and play (or tidy your room).

5 Roll out the dough on a floured surface until roughly 1/8-inch thick.

6 Cut out the biscuits using a bone-shaped cookie cutter.

7 Place on baking trays lined with parchment paper and chill in the fridge for 30 minutes.

8 Preheat oven to 325°F.

9 Bake for 10–15 minutes, or until just brown.

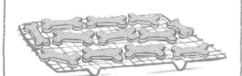

10 Transfer to a cooling rack.

11 Once cool, sandwich together pairs of biscuits with peanut butter.

Ingredients

1 tbsp soft butter
3 ripe bananas
¼ cup honey
⅓ cup brown sugar
½ cup olive oil
2 medium eggs
⅔ cup all-purpose flour
½ cup whole wheat flour
2 tsp baking powder
Extra honey for topping

Makes 8–10 slices

Honey "Hananah" Cake

This is my friend Hannah's favorite cake! We often make it together and then eat it together, so I like to think of it as honey "Hananah" cake. This is quite a deep cake, so if you're not sure if it's cooked all the way through, just pop a skewer through the middle. If it comes out clean, the cake should be cooked. After a few days it's best toasted with a little honey drizzled over the top.

Method

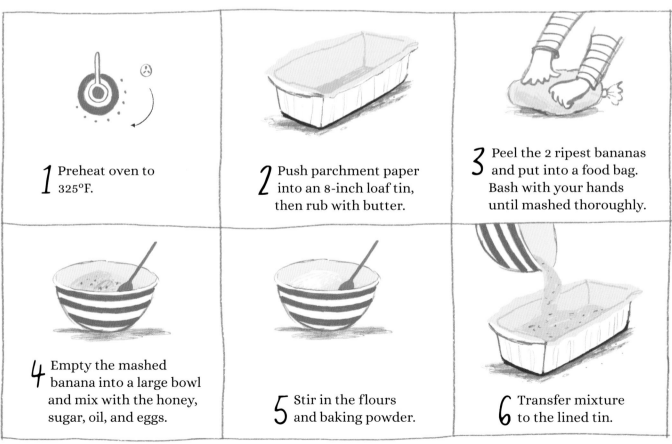

1 Preheat oven to 325°F.

2 Push parchment paper into an 8-inch loaf tin, then rub with butter.

3 Peel the 2 ripest bananas and put into a food bag. Bash with your hands until mashed thoroughly.

4 Empty the mashed banana into a large bowl and mix with the honey, sugar, oil, and eggs.

5 Stir in the flours and baking powder.

6 Transfer mixture to the lined tin.

7 Peel and slice the third banana and place gently on top.

8 Bake for 60 minutes. Use a skewer to test that it's cooked through, then transfer the cake to a cooling rack.

9 Once cool, slice into pieces and drizzle with extra honey.

Super-Sweet Brownies

If you like chocolate, these brownies are for you. They are super-gooey and rich and soft, and the sweet potato adds an extra layer of texture and sweetness. You can use dark or milk chocolate for this recipe and can also add lots of extras, such as dried fruit, chocolate chunks, or chopped nuts.

Ingredients

1 large sweet potato
6 tbsp butter
4 oz chocolate
1 cup granulated sugar
2 medium eggs
1 tsp vanilla extract
¾ cup all-purpose
    flour
1 tbsp cocoa powder
½ tsp baking powder
A pinch of salt

Makes 9 brownies

Method

1 Preheat oven to 400°F. Bake the sweet potato for 45 minutes, then allow to cool. (You can do this ahead of time.)

2 Scoop out the sweet potato flesh and mash in a bowl until smooth. (You can use a fork or stick blender to do this.)

3 Line an 8-inch square tin with parchment paper.

4 Turn oven down to 325°F.

5 Melt the butter in a saucepan over a low heat. Break the chocolate into pieces and add to the saucepan, stirring continuously until smooth.

6 Pour the chocolate mix over the sweet potato. Add the sugar, eggs, and vanilla and mix together.

7 Add the flour, cocoa, baking powder, and salt and mix until smooth.

8 Pour into tin and bake for 30 minutes.

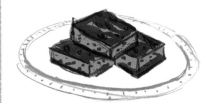

9 Carefully remove from tin and cool on a cooling rack, then cut into 9 squares.

Valentine Upside-Down Cake

Ingredients

1 can of sliced peaches

A handful of frozen raspberries

½ cup soft butter

¾ cup brown sugar

2 tbsp honey

1 tsp vanilla extract

1 large egg

⅔ cup plain yogurt

1 ½ cups all-purpose flour

2 tsp baking powder

Extra honey to top

Makes 8–10 slices

Let your friends and family know that you love them by giving them a big slice of valentine upside-down cake and a hug! This cake is fun to make because you don't know what it will look like until you turn it over after baking to reveal the pattern on top. You can use different fruits and make whatever design you like—feel free to experiment!

Method

1 Preheat oven to 350°F.

2 Push parchment paper into an 8-inch loaf tin, then rub with butter.

3 Arrange the peach slices and raspberries on the parchment paper in your heart design.

4 In a large bowl, beat the butter, sugar, honey, and vanilla until smooth.

5 Beat in the egg and yogurt. Gently mix in the flour and baking powder until smooth.

6 Carefully spoon the mixture on top of the fruit in the tin. Bake for 40–45 minutes, or until a skewer through the middle comes out clean.

7 Once baked, wait for 10 minutes and then turn the cake over with a plate. Now you can drizzle it all over with honey.

Ingredients

½ cup soft unsalted butter

⅔ cup granulated sugar

3 medium eggs

1 ⅓ cups all-purpose flour

2 tsp vanilla extract

1 tsp baking powder

½ cup raspberry jam

Powdered sugar to dust

Makes 12 buns

Victoria Sandwich Buns

Sometimes the classics are the best. People in the UK have been baking this cake for many, many years. If you know anyone from there, I'm sure they LOVE a Victoria sandwich cake. Try a Victoria sandwich yourself with these mini versions that are baked with jam in the middle.

Method

1 Preheat oven to 350°F.

2 Line a 12-hole cupcake tin with cupcake wrappers.

3 Cream together the butter and sugar until pale.

4 Beat in 1 egg.

5 Stir in half the flour.

6 Beat in another egg.

7 Stir in the other half of the flour and the baking powder.

8 Finally, beat in the third egg and the vanilla extract until smooth.

9 Put a tablespoon of batter into each wrapper, add half a teaspoon of jam, then put another spoonful of batter over the top.

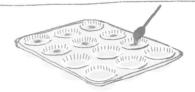

10 Bake for 20 minutes. Leave to cool, then dust with powdered sugar.

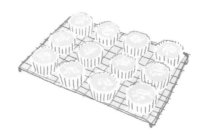

Zingy Cake Squares

Lemons are sour, but when they're used in a mix with a little sugar, they can make a sweet and zingy cake. Zesting lemons can be tricky, so if you want to leave this out, you can use a few drops of lemon oil instead.

Ingredients

Cake

2 lemons

2 cups granulated sugar

½ cup soft unsalted butter

½ cup vegetable oil

3 medium eggs

2 ½ cups all-purpose flour

2 tsp baking powder

¼ cup chia seeds

Icing

¼ cup chia seeds

Juice from 2 lemons above

1 cup unsalted cashew nuts

1 very ripe mango

¼ cup powdered sugar

Makes 16 squares

Method

1 Soak the cashews in hot water and set aside to cool. Preheat oven to 325°F.

2 Grease and dust an 8-inch square tin with a little flour.

3 Zest the lemons with a fine grater, then save the lemons for the icing.

4 Beat the sugar, butter, oil, and zest until light and fluffy. (You will need to use a mixer.)

5 Add the eggs one at a time and beat in.

6 Beat the flour, baking powder, and chia seeds into the mix.

7 Add the mix to the tin and smooth the top.

8 Bake for 40 minutes.

9 Allow to cool in the tin for 10 minutes, then turn out onto a cooling rack.

10 Juice the lemons and pour into a blender. Drain the cashew nuts.

11 Peel the mango and chop it into chunks, carefully removing the stone, then add the pieces to the blender.

12 Add the powdered sugar and cashew nuts and blend until smooth. Then add the chia seeds.

13 Spread the icing on the cake once cooled. Cut the cake into squares.

Ingredients

3 cups self-rising flour

1 tsp baking powder

¼ cup granulated sugar

6 tbsp butter (diced)

¾ cup milk

Some extra milk

A jar of strawberry jam

Makes 18 scones

Heart-Stopper Scones

These silky scones look stylish and yet they're so easy to make. The red jam is perfect for the hearts, and the scones are baked with the jam already in, so they're ready to eat as they are. If you want your family and friends to feel even *more* loved, serve with a blob of yogurt and a strawberry, then dust with a little powdered sugar. Divine!

Method

1 Preheat oven to 350°F.

2 In a bowl, rub the butter, flour, baking powder, and sugar until the mixture looks like breadcrumbs.

3 Pour in the milk.

4 Mix until it just forms a dough and let it sit for 10 minutes.

5 On a floured surface, roll out the dough until roughly ¼-inch thick.

6 Cut out scones using a 2-inch round cookie cutter.

7 In half of the scones, cut out a heart using a small heart-shaped cookie cutter.

8 Brush a little milk onto each scone. Place a heart scone on top of each complete scone and fill the hole with jam (not quite to the top).

9 Transfer to a lined baking tray and bake for 15 minutes.

10 Leave to cool on a cooling rack before eating. (The jam will be very, very hot.)

Ingredients

2 Granny Smith apples

4 tbsp water

1 tsp ground cinnamon

A handful of frozen
    raspberries

¼ cup all-purpose flour

3 tbsp whole wheat flour

2 tbsp almond meal

3 tbsp butter (diced)

⅓ cup brown sugar

⅓ cup rolled oats

Makes 4 pots

Golden Crumble Pots

My no. 1 favorite dessert! As a kid I loved climbing trees
to collect the apples for making a crumble. I like these treats
because I can have one all to myself with some custard, ice
cream, or yogurt. What will you have with yours?

Method

1 Peel and core the apples, then cut into small cubes.

2 Add the apple and cinnamon to a saucepan with 4 tbsp water.

3 Gently heat on the lowest heat for 15 minutes, until the apple is just starting to get soft at the edges.

4 Spoon the apple and frozen raspberries into 4 oven-proof ramekins.

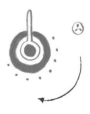

5 Preheat oven to 400°F.

6 Put the flours, almond meal, and butter in a bowl and rub until the mixture resembles breadcrumbs.

7 Add the sugar and oats and rub these through.

8 Sprinkle a little of the mix on top of each crumble until it is all used.

9 Bake for 25 minutes, until golden on top.

Christmas Cookie Baubles

These baubles are the best kind of decoration—they make your Christmas tree look so beautiful *and* you can eat them! You can decorate the cookies as you wish and can even color the icing. I like to use a toothpick to marble a little colored icing over the white icing. Just be careful not to eat them all before Christmas Day arrives!

Ingredients

Cookies

⅓ cup butter

1 tbsp honey

¼ cup brown sugar

½ tsp orange extract

⅔ cup all-purpose flour

⅓ cup bread flour

A pinch of baking powder

2 tsp pumpkin pie spice

½ tsp ground cinnamon

1 small egg

Royal icing

1 egg white

1 ¾ cups powdered sugar

1 tsp lemon juice

Makes 20–24 cookies

Method

1 Melt the butter, honey, sugar, and orange extract, then set aside to cool slightly.

2 Combine the flours, baking powder, and spices in a mixing bowl.

3 Once the wet mixture is cooled, lightly whisk in the egg.

4 Stir this into the flour mixture. (It will seem very wet.)

5 Pour into a bag and seal. Chill in the fridge until it forms a firm dough.

6 Roll out to roughly 1/8-inch thickness and cut out with a 2-inch round cookie cutter. Use the end of a pen top to make a little hole in the top of each cookie.

7 Put on lined cookie sheets and then chill in the fridge for 30 minutes.

8 Preheat oven to 340°F.

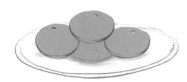

9 Bake each tray of cookies for 12 minutes. Allow to cool before removing from tray.

10 Whisk all the icing ingredients together until the icing is thick enough to leave a line on the surface of the mixture for 10 seconds when the whisk is lifted.

11 Scoop into a piping bag and pipe onto each cookie. You can add edible decorations on top if you wish.

12 Allow icing to dry until hard before threading the ribbon and hanging on the tree.

David Atherton is the winner of *The Great British Baking Show* 2019. Before applying to be a contestant on the show, he worked as an international health advisor, spending time in UK Aid–funded hospitals overseas. As well as being passionate about cooking, he is a fitness enthusiast and is always looking for another craft to master. *Bake, Make, and Learn to Cook* is his first book for children.

Rachel Stubbs is a London-based illustrator who loves observing human behavior and interaction. While earning a master's degree in children's book illustration, she rediscovered the joy of drawing from life in her sketchbook, and she loves nothing more than getting outside to draw in her local parks, cafés, and museums. She was awarded the Sebastian Walker Award for illustration in 2017, and her debut picture book, *My Red Hat,* was published in 2020.